The Children's Book of Books 1999

In celebration of

WORLD BOOK DAY

Published in association with
HarperCollins*Publishers*.

The Children's Book of Books 1999 has been compiled and
produced by HarperCollins Publishers.

Editor: Domenica de Rosa
HarperCollins Publishers Ltd, 77-85 Fulham Palace Road,
Hammersmith, London, W6 8JB.
First published 1999

World Book Day 1999 is an initiative sponsored by booksellers and publishers and supported by the printing industry. It is run in association with the BBC.

The following organisations have contributed to World Book Day 1999, through financial sponsorship or support in kind. They include The Booksellers' Association of Great Britain and Ireland, the Publishers Association, the Basic Skills Agency, Book Tokens Ltd, the Department for Education and Employment, and the Department of Trade and Industry.

The organisers would also like to thank:

Publishers
Major contributors: HarperCollins Publishers Ltd; Hodder Headline plc; Little, Brown & Company; Macmillan Publishers Ltd; Penguin Books Ltd; Random House UK Ltd; Transworld Publishers Ltd. Other contributors: A&C Black (Publishers) Ltd; BBC Worldwide; Bloomsbury Publishing plc; Andre Deutsch Ltd; Egmont Children's Books; Faber & Faber; Oxford University Press; Scholastic Ltd; Simon and Schuster; Usborne Publishing; Walker Books Ltd; The Watts Group; Yale University Press

Booksellers
Most booksellers in the UK and Ireland are supporting World Book Day through the cost of redeeming free £1 book vouchers. The organisers would like to thank the following in particular: Bertrams the Book Wholesaler; Books etc; Bookland; Borders; Dillons the Bookstore; Easons; Gardners Books Ltd; Hammicks Bookshops Ltd; James Thin; Lomond Books; Mahers the Booksellers; Methuen; Ottakers; Sussex Stationers; Wesley Owen; WH Smith plc; THE Books; Waterstone's.

Printers and Manufacturers
Bath Press; Borregaard Hellefos A/S; Caledonian International Book Manufacturing Ltd; Clays Ltd; William Clowes Ltd; Concise Cover Printers Ltd; Creative Print & Design Group; Enso Publication Papers Ltd; Farringdon Printers Ltd; Iggesund Board Suppliers; Letterpart; Mackays of Chatham; Martins the Printers Ltd; Metsa Serla; Norske Skog Ltd; Robert Horne Paper; Saxon Photolitho Ltd; Shalefield, White Quill Press.

Distribution
HarperCollins Ltd; Bertrams the Book Wholesaler; Easons; Gardners Books Ltd; THE Books.

The organisers would also like to thank all those supporters who have contributed to the campaign since The Children's Book of Books 1999 and The Grown Ups' Book of Books went to press.

Foreword

Hi and welcome to *The Children's Book of Books 1999!*

This book has been published especially for World Book Day which takes place every year on 23rd April, Shakespeare's birthday.

In the UK and Ireland, millions of children and young people will be given a free £1 voucher which they can exchange for *The Children's Book of Books 1999*. And, to help out in other parts of the world where books are in short supply, many schools will be raising money to support Book Aid International, the charity that donates books to schools in developing countries.

The Children's Book of Books 1999 is more than just a book, it's a whole bookshelf packed with some top extracts to give you a taste of the very best writing around.

It includes favourites like Anne Fine, Robert Leeson, Paula Danziger, Michael Morpurgo, Charles Causley and Valerie Bloom, exciting new writers like Narinder Dhami and Ian Whybrow, as well as classic poems from the legendary A.A. Milne and Ted Hughes.

Inside there's something for everyone. So if you only read one book on World Book Day, make sure it's *The Children's Book of Books 1999*.

Curl up and enjoy!

Katy Hill

Contents

Animal Magic

Rules for my Dog

by Geraldine Taylor

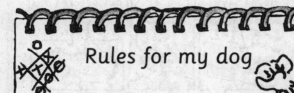

Rules for my dog

Don't sit under my chair when I'm
eating my dinner and make smells.
Everyone looks at me and says
"Stop it!" and it's not fair!

Don't keep putting your wet nose
in my pocket – my mouse doesn't
like it.

Don't dig up Dad's best rose trees.
I don't need you to help me find
my worms.

Don't lick my knees.
It's horrible.
Go and lick my sister.

Mr Croc Rocks!

by Frank Rodgers

Mr Croc Gets Fit

by Frank Rodgers

Usborne Farmyard Tales

by Heather Amery
illustrated by Stephen Cartwright

This is Mrs. Boot, the farmer. She has two
children called Poppy and Rusty.

"Where are you going today?" asks Poppy.
"To the old railway station," says Mrs. Boot.

"It's the train. It's coming," says Mrs. Boot.
"Look, it's a steam train," says Poppy. "How exciting."

The train chugs slowly down the track. "Doesn't the old station look good now?" says Poppy.

From The Old Steam Train

ANIMORPHS

by K. A. Applegate

I did it Monday morning in my locker at school. I turned into a lizard.

I started to focus for the morphing. I remembered the way we had caught the lizard the night before last. We'd spotted it with a torch, and Cassie had put a bucket over it so it couldn't get away.

It had been fairly creepy, just touching it to acquire its DNA pattern. Now I was going to become it.

Things began to happen very fast. It was like falling. Like falling off a skyscraper and taking for ever to hit the ground.

And then the lizard brain kicked in.

Fear! Trapped! Run! Run! Rruunrunrun!

Go to the light! I ordered my new body. But the body was afraid of the light. It was terrified.

Go to the light! I screamed inside my head. And suddenly I was there.

In the bright light I realized how bad the lizard eyes were. I couldn't make sense of what I was seeing. Everything was shattered and twisted around. Down was up and up was down.

I tried to think. Come on, Jake. You have eyes on the side of your head now. They don't focus together. They see different things. Deal with it.

I tried to make sense of the pictures, using this knowledge, but they were still a mess. It seemed to take me for ever to figure it out. One eye was looking down the hall to the left. The other was looking down the hall to the right. I was upside down, gripping the side of the locker, which was like a long, grey field that wouldn't end.

Suddenly I was off and running. Straight down the wall. Zoom! Then on level floor. Zoom! The ground flew past. It was like being strapped on to a crazy, out-of-control missile.

Then my lizard brain sensed the spider. It was a strange thing, like I wasn't sure if I saw the spider, or heard it, or smelled it, or tasted it on my flicking lizard tongue, or just suddenly knew it was there.

I took off after it, racing at a million miles an hour before I could even think about stopping. My legs were a blur, they moved so fast.

The spider ran. I ran after it. I was faster.

Noooooooo! I screamed inside my head.

WELCOME TO PET HOTEL

by Mandy Archer

Join Sophie and Becky Ashford at Tangletrees Pet Hotel — an amazing holiday centre for animals, large and small.

"Girls, can you come here, please!" hollered Mrs Fitzgerald from the kitchen. Up to her arms in pizza base mixture, she was right in the middle of preparing Saturday lunch. "Girls!"

Becky and Sophie finally emerged from the garden to answer their childminder.

"Can you cheer up Albert? Charlie's stolen his dog basket again," Mrs Fitzgerald sighed. "Every time I turf the little devil out, he slinks back into it."

On hearing his name the retriever sat bolt upright in the wicker basket. Albert, the girls' Westie, was beside him, growling irritably. But Charlie didn't seem to notice - as he panted excitedly it even looked as if he was smiling.

"Poor Bertie. Come and play with us," laughed Sophie. "I've made him a much nicer new bed in the front room, but he won't have it." She held out her arms to the terrier, who gave up on his basket and took an impressive running jump towards her.

"I just think Charlie is finding it strange getting used to his temporary home," sympathised Becky. But, when she bent down to play with the retriever's ears, she had to admit he looked far from unhappy.

"Well, he'll be all right soon, but we will all have to work hard on perfecting our animal skills," pointed out Mrs Fitzgerald. "Every pet that comes to stay will be feeling a bit vulnerable and uneasy when they are first checked into Pet Hotel, won't they?"

Becky and Sophie's dad, Dan Ashford, had been working with Mrs Fitzgerald to convert her home into a holiday pet centre. The renovations to Tangletrees were now well under way, and Mrs Fitzgerald and her clan of pets had moved themselves into the Ashford house until the building work was done. It had taken a lot of hard work to devise a totally animal-friendly centre and, as it got closer to opening, Becky and Sophie were growing more and more excited.

Sophie transferred the little white dog to Becky's lap, where he gradually calmed down and dropped off to sleep. "I think most animals seem to cheer up when you show them love," smiled Becky.

BANG!

A thundering crash shook the room from outside, sending Albert up in the air in fright. He flew off Becky's lap and into the basket Charlie had abandoned during the commotion. The girls scrambled to the back door as Dan tramped through, covered in grass cuttings and mud. Mrs Fitzgerald's two stout ginger toms scooted through the door behind him, almost knocking the girls' dad off balance.

"Blast!" he swore, yanking his boots off. Eventually his right welly gave way, sending him backwards on to his bottom. "Aargh!"

"What on earth was that noise?" cried Mrs Fitzgerald.

"The engine on the lawnmower's blown up," Dan frowned. "I just don't think I'm cut out for this country-life business." Eventually he managed to peel off his woolly hat and waxed jacket. He sat down at the kitchen table, sinking an elbow into one of Mrs Fitzgerald's pizza bases by mistake.

"Rubbish!" announced Mrs Fitzgerald. "Things will be much easier when you've served your notice out and get into things here full time." She discreetly tried to pull the dough out from underneath Dan's arm, but he looked so gloomy she decided to leave it where it was.

"Come on, Dad, you're doing a great job," soothed Becky. She could understand exactly how daunting all this must be for him.

Dan had two weeks to go until he gave up his city job to concentrate on the pet centre. In the meantime, he was only able to help in the evenings and at weekends. Becky squeezed her dad's hand. He was looking more tired than ever.

"Becky's right, of course," agreed Mrs Fitzgerald. "You've just got to relax."

"I know, I know," Dan mumbled. "I just feel that my stress levels seem to be going up instead of down!"

Sophie could see her dad was about to launch into a lengthy speech, but he was distracted by a gentle neighing sound. The back door was nudged open to reveal Mrs Fitzgerald's Shetland pony, Billy, poking his head into the room and whinnying in delight. Half the washing line was wrapped round his chestnut head and body.

"Now I've got a pony in my kitchen!" Dad cried in desperation.

"Oh dear," sighed Mrs Fitzgerald. "It looks like he's doubling as a clothes horse."

Becky's heart skipped a beat. She had only been grooming him seconds ago. "His rope must have come loose," she said apologetically. "Sorry, Dad! It won't happen again – ever."

"You must be careful, Becks, because Billy could have hurt himself," Dan warned.

Becky tore outside to tie up the stray pony and remove the now dirty laundry. She was annoyed with herself for her carelessness. Her mind kept settling on one terrible thought – if they were finding it so hard to cope with their own animals, how was Pet Hotel ever going to work?

LITTLE WOLF'S HAUNTED HALL FOR SMALL HORRORS

by Ian Whybrow

Dear Mum and Dad,

Please please PLEEEEZ don't be so grrrish. It's not fair Dad keeps saying, "GET A MOVE ON LAZYBONES, OPEN YOUR SCHOOL QUICK." Just because he has fangache, I bet, boo shame. Today I will do news 1st, then cheery pics for him after.

Yeller and me and Stubbs are trying and trying. Paws crossed we open soonly. But did you forget our 1 big problem I told you about before? I will tell you wunce more. It is the ghost of Uncle Bigbad. He is fine, in a dead way, but he keeps being ~~orkwood~~ nasty, saying do this and do that or no more haunting from me. Just because he knows we *neeeed* him for our School Spirit.

21

Here is a pic of Haunted Hall, the scaryest school in the world (opening soonly):

I am not drawing a pic of Uncle Bigbad. Because 1) he is too crool, and 2) you cannot see ghosts, only after midnight (get it?)

I will draw me and Yeller, my best friend and cuz, instead:

𝑎 is just us being normal (Yeller is the loud 1).

𝑏 is us dressed up as bossy Heads saying, "No chewing in class," ect.

Now I will do Stubbs the crowchick:

𝑎 is him being all proud of 2 new feathers.

𝑏 is him doing looptheloops in his glowmask.

    And now just 1 more: a Small Horror of Haunted Hall in his spooksuit. Guess who? Yes, Smellybreff, my baby bruv, going sob sob I want my mummy. (Only joking, he likes it here really.)

    Yours cubly,
    L Wolf
    (son and Co-Head)

THE JEWEL

by William Mayne

Buff, a toad under the grass with his heels out and his thumbs in, caught Black Fly.

"Knees in, wings back, please," said Buff to Black Fly, trapped on his long tongue.

"Buzz," said Black Fly. It had not happened to him before; he did not wish it now. Buff swallowed him. Black Fly did not fold his wings or bend his legs. Maggots are not raised civil any more, thought Buff, and I've not felt well all day.

Striped Fly came by, Homberson Bomberson. "Don't catch me, I sting," he buzzed, stripy, noisy, hot in the sun.

Buff lived in a little garden, where a cottage stood. The garden was quite bare. All that could go into the pot had been eaten now. There was no shelter. Homberson Bomberson hung over his head and buzzed. For Buff it was too hot. He had a mortal headache now.

He crawled through the cottage doorway and sat on the cold stone. He was poorly, but the people were in poverty; the woman and her children licked their fingers to live.

The sun set. The children lay down hungry. Buff spread his elbows and put his hand on his aching head.

The woman of the cottage said, "You'd better be outside; no-one has food here," and lifted him out to the cool dark.

Buff lay there all night, his head larger and larger with pain. In the morning Homberson Bomberson came to buzz.

Buff crept to the shade of the kitchen corner. Sadness was in the cottage, the people were in sorrow.

"Today's joy," they said, "is that we're poorer still tomorrow."

At night they led Buff outside. What can tomorrow bring? he thought. Nothing eats us toads. We live in vain.

By morning he was too weak to move. The kind but starving people put him in the darkest corner of the house and poured cold water on his pained head, all they had.

Homberson Bomberson cried, "Come and join in the fun."

Buff, with his hand on his ears, wondered how he could take his aching head right off, just like that. All afternoon he pulled and pushed. As the sun began to set he felt his skull begin to move. As shadows fell the joint above his mouth came loose. As darkness came around, a hard thing dropped on his tongue, and all his pain was over.

Just follow nature, he thought. I knew it in my bones. He laid the hard thing down and crept outside.

Through the house grew a glow of light. The woman and her children thought it was some dream of being dead.

They found the reason on the floor. It was the jewel from the head of Buff, his pain, the pain of every toad.

The shining stone brought food and joy to the cottage and dry garden. The children made for Buff a sheltered house and let him wander in and out. When daylight came he sat in his new house.

"Feeling better then," said Homberson Bomberson, flying low and loud and much too stripy.

"Yes," said Buff. With his tongue he gathered in the stripe and noise of Homberson Bomberson, and closed his mouth on him.

"Knees in, wings back," said Homberson Bomberson, too surprised to sting.

A pleasure, thought Buff, to meet someone well brought up. It's peaceful now. And tomorrow will be better still.

Creatures

ONCE I CAUGHT A FISH ALIVE

by Louise Cooper

"It is bigger," Gemma said uneasily. "In fact, I'd say it's grown about three centimetres since yesterday."

Paul didn't answer. He dared not, because he agreed with her and didn't want to acknowledge it. The fish gazed back through the glass and fanned its tail and fins lazily. They had both been trying to outstare it, but had found they couldn't; the fish had a patience and determination that was unnerving, and it simply wouldn't look away. Paul thought: It's challenging us. It knows we're getting the wind up, and it's enjoying every moment. What sort of creature have I landed myself with?

The Legend of Luke

by Brian Jacques

(Abridged extract)

Leaving the safety of Redwall Abbey behind him, Martin the Warrior mouse has returned to the place of his birth, the Northland Shore. An encounter with an ancient warrior, Vurg, has led Martin and his companions, Gonff the Mousethief, Trimp, Dinny, Folgrim, Furmo and the Guosim shrews to the hazardous Tall Rocks and has brought them one step closer to discovering the truth about Martin's father, Luke...

The strong, slender ropes snaked out and up. Three iron grapples clanked simultaneously into the stone crevices. Honeysuckle was secured safely; she bobbed up and down alongside the rocks, with the slack lines allowing her to ride easily on the swells.

Vurg took a deep breath. Cupping his paws around his mouth he called out in a quavery voice, 'Ahoy the Arfship! Ahoy there, can you 'ear me?'

There was no answer. Furmo the shrew felt recovered enough to roar out in a thunderous baritone, 'Ahoy Arfship, 'tis Vurg an' some company. Ahoooooy!'

Martin just had time to pull the ship to one side, avoiding a hefty rope ladder with timber rungs. It came down out of the rocks and clattered to the deck.

Gonff stared in puzzlement at Vurg. 'Who are we shouting to an' wot's an Arfship, mate?'

On a ledge above them, a hare appeared. He looked as ancient as Vurg, older in fact. Shaking a tremulous paw at Vurg, he called down, 'Where in the name of my auntie's apron have you been, wot? I've been sittin' up here like a blinkin' sickly seagull, worryin' about you, sah! Now y'come sailin' up here, pretty as y' please, in charge of this jolly old rats' regatta, wot!'

Vurg mounted the rope ladder with Trimp's assistance, arguing with the hare as he climbed up to the ledge. 'Oh give yore flappin' jaws a rest, Beau. These creatures are friends, they brought me back here from Northshore. Which is more'n I can say for you. I'd grow whiskers t'me footpaws waitin' on you t'come an' fetch me, y'great flop-eared, bag-bellied, droopy-pawed rock rabbit!'

The old hare's ears stood up indignantly as

he helped Vurg onto the ledge. 'Hah! Rock rabbit is it, you blather-bottomed old dodderer, wot, wot? I've had a barnacle casserole bubblin' here for two confounded days waitin' for you. Bad form, sah! I was goin't'make a plum pudden, too, but I flippin' well ain't now. So you can go an' jolly well whistle f'your blinkin' supper for all I care an' I hope the casserole keeps you awake all night. Ungrateful bounder!'

Martin popped his head over the ledge. 'When you two creatures have stopped arguing, would you mind moving aside? We've got a ship's crew to get up this ladder.'

Vurg and Beau led them up through a perfectly round tunnel in the rock. They emerged on the other side amid the massed pinnacles and stood gazing up in open-mouthed awe at the sight that greeted them. Beau managed to make an elegant leg and bowed slightly. 'Welcome to the vessel Arfship!'

Jammed between the column they stood upon and the one immediately next to it, was half a ship. High overhead them it stood, lodged between both pinnacles, more than two thirds of the way up. From midships to forward end it was wedged firmly, a huge rusting iron spike at its forepeak driven into the rock by some tremendous force. The thing had once been red, but now, through seasons of harsh weather, seaspray, sun and rain, it was faded to a rose-pink hue. Dinny's voice cut the silence. 'Well fill my tunnel! Arf a ship oop in ee air!'

Ascending another rope ladder, they climbed up to the odd habitation. Trimp stared around in astonishment at the immensity of it all. It was like being in some great chamber. Timbered bulkheads with holes for oarports let in the light, as did the opened hatch covers high above them.

Furmo's voice echoed spectrally in the vast space as Honeysuckle's crew walked through it wide-eyed. 'An' this is supposed t'be only arf a ship! I tell ye mates, could you imagine it afore it was broken, with the other arf attached? It must've been like a floatin' village. I wager there wasn't anythin' that size ever sailed the seas!'

Vurg nodded his head. 'Oh, but there was, an' this is what's left of it. See through those open hatch covers? There's another deck above this an' another one above that again. You're lookin' through three decks up t'the main one, which, if y'count it, makes four altogether. We keeps the 'atches open to give light an' battens 'em down in bad weather. Up these stairs is the forward cabins. Come on, I'll show ye!'

Martin shook his head as he passed rows of benches with chains hanging from them and long, broken oars banging through the ports. They looked well worn from constant use. 'Beau, was this a slave ship?'

'Indeed it was, old lad. The foulest, most evil vessel that ever plied the oceans. Now 'tis our home; we named it Arfship. Actually, 'twould have been Half Ship if I'd had me way, but the others called it Arfship, so Arfship it is, wot. Come an' eat now, questions later, that's the drill!'

Following him up the ornately carved staircase, they entered a roomy cabin with its skylights thrown open. It was a complete living area. Tables, chairs, bunks and cupboards were all about, clean and neat. Two mice, old and grey, were working at a table next to a big glowing stove with its smokepipe thrusting though the edge of the skylight.

Vurg introduced them. 'This is all of us left from those who sailed off long ago from the North Shores. Myself, Dulam and Denno.'

The mouse called Denno went straight to Martin and took the warrior's face gently in both his flour-dusted paws. 'No need t' tell ole Denno who you are. I know. Luke's son, Martin — couldn't be no other beast. Yore the spittin' image o' the great Luke, though you got yore mother Sayna's eyes.'

Martin shook visibly, blinking his eyes hard. 'You knew my mother?'

Denno nodded. 'Course I did, an' a prettier, more gentle creature there never was. I knew em all, Martin, everybeast. But we've got all night to talk of that. Sit down and rest now, the food will be ready soon.'

After the tables were pushed together and set, they sat down. Martin decided that the time had come. 'Tell me, Vurg, what became of my father, Luke the Warrior?'

Beau rose stiffly and went to a cupboard. He returned to the table with a large, dusty volume. 'Tis all within these pages, Martin, everything, as best as the four of us can recall. We spent many a winter an' autumn night recordin' the entire tales; 'twas a joint work. D'y'know, I thought it might be found by somebeast, long after we were gone. But fate an' fortunes've smiled on us, laddie buck. There's food 'n' drink on the table an' a long night ahead of us, wot! Here, Denno, you young whippersnapper, you can understand your own writing best. Read the journal to our friends, there's a good chap!'

Denno polished a tiny pair of glasses.

Perching them on his nose, he looked over at Martin.

'I was the scribe y'see. Right, let's start at the beginning. I 'ope you like the title, 'tis called, "In the wake of the Red Ship", this being an account of Luke the Warrior, written by his friends.'

Outside, the eternal seas washed against Tall Rocks. Breezes sighed a wistful dirge about the basalt columns where seabirds wheeled and called. In the cabin, high among the pinnacles, Martin of Redwall listened as the saga of his father, Luke the Warrior, unfolded.

Life and other Heartaches

Romeo goes to a party at the home of his family's enemies, the Capulets. He sees Juliet.

Did my heart love 'til now? Forswear it, sight! For I ne'er saw true beauty till this night.

Palm to palm is holy <u>palmer</u>'s kiss.

Ay, pilgrim, lips that they must use in prayer.

Have not saints lips, and holy palmers too?

palmer – pilgrim

O then, let lips do what hands do.

Move not, while my prayers' effect I take.

Then have my lips the sin that they have took?

Thus from my lips by thine, my sin is purg'd.

Sin from my lips? Give me my sin again.

WHEN HITLER STOLE PINK RABBIT

by Judith Kerr

The train was almost empty and they had a whole compartment to themselves until a lady with a basket got in at the next station. Anna could hear a sort of shuffling inside the basket — there must be something alive in it. She tried to catch Max's eye to see if he had heard it too, but he was frowning out of the window. Anna began to feel bad-tempered too and to remember that her head ached and that her boots were still wet from last night's rain.

"When do we get to the frontier?" she asked.

"I don't know," said Mama. "Not for a while yet."

"In about an hour, d'you think?" asked Anna.

"You never stop asking questions," said Max, although it was none of his business. "Why can't you shut up?"

"Why can't you?" said Anna. She was bitterly hurt and cast around for something wounding to say. At last she came out with, "I wish I had a sister!"

"I wish I didn't!" said Max.

"Mama…!" wailed Anna.

"Oh, for goodness' sake, stop it!" cried Mama. "Haven't we got enough to worry about?" She was clutching her bag and peering into it every so often to see if the passports were still there.

Anna wriggled crossly in her seat. Everybody was horrible. The lady with the basket had produced a large chunk of bread with some ham and was eating it. No one said anything for a long time. Then the train began to slow down.

"Excuse me," said Mama, "but are we coming to the Swiss frontier?"

The lady with the basket munched and shook her head.

"There, you see!" said Anna to Max. "Mama is asking questions too!"

Max rolled his eyes up to heaven. Anna wanted to kick him, but Mama would have noticed.

The train stopped and started again, stopped and started again. Each time Mama asked if it was the frontier, and each time the lady with the basket shook her head. At last when the train slowed down yet again the lady with the basket said, "I dare say we're coming to it now."

They waited in silence while the train stood in the station. Anna could hear voices and the doors of other compartments opening and shutting. Then footsteps in the corridor. Then the door of their own compartment slid open and the passport inspector came in. He had a uniform rather like a ticket inspector and a large brown moustache.

He looked at the passport of the lady with the basket, nodded, stamped it with a little rubber stamp, and gave it back to her. Then he turned to Mama. Mama handed him the passports and smiled. But the hand with which she was holding her handbag was squeezing it into terrible contortions. The man examined the passports. Then he looked at Mama to see if it was the same face as on the passport photograph, then at Max and then at Anna. Then he got out his rubber stamp. Then he remembered something and looked at the passports again. Then at last he stamped them and gave them back to Mama.

"Pleasant journey," he said as he opened the door of the compartment.

Nothing had happened. Max had frightened her all for nothing.

"There, you see...!" cried Anna, but Mama gave her such a look that she stopped.

The passport inspector closed the door behind him.

"We are still in Germany," said Mama.

Anna could feel herself blushing scarlet. Mama put the passports back in the bag. There was silence. Anna could hear whatever it was scuffling in the basket, the lady munching another piece of bread and ham, doors opening and shutting further and further along the train. It seemed to last for ever.

Then the train started, rolling a few hundred yards and stopped again. More opening and shutting of doors, this time more quickly. Voices saying, "Customs... anything to declare ...?" A different man came into the compartment. Mama and the lady both said they had nothing to declare and he made a mark with chalk on all their luggage, even on the lady's basket. Another wait, then a whistle and at last they started again. This time the train gathered speed and went on chugging steadily through the countryside.

After a long time Anna asked, "Are we in Switzerland yet?"

"I think so. I'm not sure," said Mama.

The lady with the basket stopped chewing.

"Oh yes," she said comfortably, "this is Switzerland now – this is my country."

It was marvellous.

"Switzerland!" said Anna. "We're really in Switzerland!"

"About time too!" said Max and grinned.

Mama put the bag down on the seat beside her and smiled and smiled.

"Well!" she said. "Well! We'll soon be with Papa."

Anna suddenly felt quite silly and light-headed. She wanted to do or say something extraordinary but could think of nothing at all – so she turned to the Swiss lady and said, "Excuse me, but what have you got in your basket?"

"That's my mogger," said the lady in her soft country voice.

For some reason this was terribly funny. Anna, biting back her laughter, glanced at Max and found that he too was almost in convulsions.

"What's a ... what's a mogger?" she asked as the lady folded back the lid of the basket, and before anyone could answer there was a screech of "Meeee", and the head of a scruffy black tomcat appeared out of the opening.

At this Anna and Max could not contain

themselves. They fell about with laughter.

"He answered you!" gasped Max. "You said, 'What's a mogger' and he said..."

"Meeee!" screamed Anna.

"Children, children!" said Mama, but it was no good — they could not stop laughing. They laughed at everything they saw, all the way to Zurich. Mama apologized to the lady but she said she did not mind — she knew high spirits when she saw them. Any time they looked like flagging Max only had to say "What's a mogger?" and Anna cried "Meeee!" and they were off all over again. They were still laughing on the platform in Zurich when they were looking for Papa.

Anna saw him first. He was standing by a bookstall. His face was white and his eyes were searching the crowds milling round the train.

"Papa!" she shouted. "Papa!"

He turned and saw them. And then Papa, who was always so dignified, who never did anything in a hurry, suddenly ran towards them. He put his arms round Mama and hugged her. Then he hugged Anna and Max. He hugged and hugged them all and would not let them go.

"I couldn't see you," said Papa. "I was afraid..."

"I know," said Mama.

The Awkward Bunch

by Alex Parsons

Tansy's chauffeur-driven limo glided to a halt. The chauffeur got out to open Tansy's door and she emerged from the back seat just as she'd been taught at Beverley Hills Junior High: swivel round, knees together, feet on the ground, push up, rise and smile! Her teachers would have been proud of her.

"Hi!" she said, to everyone and no one in particular. "My name is Tansy Steel." She looked in amazement at Eden and Calypso. "No one told me the grunge look was back quite so... overwhelmingly," she said.

"Well, they warned us to expect a Hollywood princess," replied Calypso crisply. "So they got something right."

Tansy scowled at the twins.

"You got a problem?" asked Eden.

"Hell no, I'm cool." Tansy dropped her voice and nodded in Cosmo's direction. "Who's nerdy-boy?"

"Cosmo!" called Calypso. "Tansy wants to get to know you better, she wants to be your special friend."

Annie's Game

by Narinder Dhami

Annie was talking to someone who wasn't there.

Jack looked across the school playground at his sister. She was nodding her head and smiling at the empty space next to her, waving her hands around as she talked. Jack wondered briefly why he was surprised. Nothing Annie did ought to surprise him any more. She was capable of anything, including having a conversation with thin air. Not that he cared what Annie was up to.

'Annie!' he called. 'Go and sit on the wall.'

Annie gave him a big smile.

'Can Sarah come with me?'

'What?' Jack turned to his sister.

'I said, "Can Sarah come with me?"'

'Sarah who?'

'Sarah Slade.' Annie pointed at the empty space next to her, a pleased look on her face.

'This is Sarah. She's my new friend. Say hello to Sarah, Jack.'

'There's no-one there,' Jack muttered.

'Yes, there is,' Annie retorted, unruffled. 'She's just invisible, that's all.'

'Of course she is,' said Jack. 'Silly me. I should have realized.'

'Don't be sarcastic, Jack.' Annie opened her eyes wide, and gave him a superior stare. 'Sarah's a time-traveller, you know. She's come to visit me from the future.'

Jack resisted a desire to bang his head against the nearest brick wall. It was a feeling he often had when he was left alone with Annie.

'Look,' he said, unable to stand any more of what threatened to be yet another of Annie's endless games, 'go over there and sit on the wall. Have you got something to read?'

Annie pouted. 'I'd rather talk to Sarah.'

Jack looked at her sternly. 'Have you got something to read?' he repeated.

Annie sighed. 'I've got two newspapers, four comics and Hamlet.'

'What do you think you're doing there, Robinson?' hissed a voice in Jack's ear.

Jack leapt a mile. Nicko was standing close beside him, grinning at him, and bouncing a football up and down with one hand.

'So,' Nicko went to squat on the wall, next to Annie. 'What's the story with this Hamlet dude then?'

'Don't sit there!' Annie yelled at the top of her lungs, pushing him away. Nicko leapt a mile as if he'd been stung, and stared at her, open-mouthed.

'Why not?'

Annie nodded at the wall next to her. 'Sarah's sitting there,' she said.

Nicko looked nervously at the empty space, then glanced at Jack. Jack shrugged, and mouthed, 'One of her daft games,' at him. Nicko squinted at him, trying to lip-read. Jack did it again, and this time Annie spotted him.

'My games are not daft,' she said haughtily. 'And anyway, this isn't a game, it's real. This is Sarah Slade.' She pointed at the empty space next to her. 'Go on, Nicko, say hello to Sarah.'

'Hello, Sarah,' Nicko said obediently. Jack kept quiet. After all that had happened so far today, he needed this like a hole in the head.

'Sarah says hi.' Annie smiled at Nicko. 'She likes you. Not like some rude people she could mention.' She looked accusingly at her brother.

Jack turned away from her. 'Leave me out of it,' he muttered.

Annie's games always drove him crazy, and he could see no reason why this one should be any different. She was always inventing games. Not ordinary, normal games like other kids made up, but complicated, imaginary projects that only she could keep track of. She wrote notes about them in exercise books and drew maps and made models, until she got bored with the current game, and started a new one. Her last game had involved a prince and a princess, a mad wizard and a blue tiger called Gerald, and she'd invented a whole imaginary country to go with it, including a made-up language which was a mixture of Spanish and English words, pronounced backwards.

'Who's Sarah, then?' Nicko asked cautiously.

'Sarah's eleven years old, and she's a time-traveller from the twenty-fifth century.' Annie beamed at him.

'Is that right?' Nicko looked over Annie's head, and winked at Jack. 'What's she doing here then?'

'She's doing a school project on the 1990s, and she's come to do some research.' Annie explained, her face serious.

'Groovy,' Nicko raised his eyebrows. 'So they still have schools in the twenty-fifth century, do they? Still, time-travelling to research a history project sounds a lot more interesting than sitting in a boring old library.'

'And she's sitting right there,' said Jack, pointing at the empty space next to Annie.

Annie nodded eagerly. She loved it when her brother took an interest in her games. Not that he often did.

'Let's see then, shall we?' Jack said with an evil grin, and he sat down next to Annie.

He wasn't quite sure what happened next. One

second he was sitting on the wall, and the next he'd overbalanced and gone heels over head onto the grass behind it, landing with a loud thud. Gasping with shock, he pulled himself upright to find Nicko and Annie peering down at him. Annie was grinning smugly and Nicko was very red in the face as if he was trying not to laugh.

'Serves you right,' Annie said cheerfully. 'I told you Sarah was sitting there.'

★   ★   ★

After they'd got home and he'd had some pizza, Jack went straight up to his bedroom to be on his own. He switched on his computer and then immediately switched it off again, feeling too restless to do anything.

'Jack?' That was his mum, calling from downstairs. 'Will you check Annie's in bed please?'

Annie's room was a tip. In the middle of it sat Annie in her pyjamas, a pair of scissors in her hand.

'Time for bed,' Jack said abruptly, not even bothering to comment on the mess as he picked his way carefully over to the window.

'Mind out, Sarah's sitting on the window-sill,' Annie said, as Jack pulled the curtains together. Jack ignored her.

He was staring at the painting set that lay on the carpet, amongst all the other model–making equipment.

'You've got my paints.' Jack felt anger welling up inside him. 'I never said you could use them.'

Annie pouted at him. 'I only borrowed them –'

'You took them from my room, and I've told you to keep out of there!' Jack yelled. He needed one place where he could get right away from Annie and everything she stood for.

Annie's face crumpled. 'I didn't think you'd mind.'

'Well, I do! Now go to bed!' Already feeling guilty, Jack grabbed the painting set, and marched out of the room.

Annie sat in bed, fat tears rolling quietly down her cheeks. She hated it when Jack got angry. However hard she tried, she always seemed to annoy him. She couldn't understand why everything she did irritated him so much. She just couldn't do anything right.

'Jack's horrible,' she sniffed. 'I hate him.'

There was a long pause. Then Annie turned to stare through the dying light at the empty space beside her, her eyes wide and surprised.

'Oh, Sarah,' she said. 'You wouldn't really do that to Jack. Would you?'

THE WRECK OF THE ZANZIBAR

by Michael Morpurgo

Today I found a turtle. I think it's called a leatherback turtle. I found one once before, but it was dead. This one has been washed up alive. Father had sent me down to collect driftwood on Rushy Bay. He said there'd be plenty about after a storm like that. He was right. I'd been there for half an hour or so heaping up the wood, before I noticed the turtle in the tideline of piled seaweed. I thought at first he was just a washed-up tree stump covered in seaweed. He was upside down on the sand. I pulled the seaweed off him. His eyes were open, unblinking. He was more dead than alive, I thought. He was massive, as long as this bed, and wider. He had a face like a two hundred year old man, wizened and wrinkled and with a gently-smiling mouth. I looked around, and there were more gulls gathering. They were silent, watching, waiting; and I knew well enough what they were waiting for. I pulled away more of the seaweed and saw that the gulls had been at him already. There was blood under his neck where the skin had been pecked. I had got there just in time.

BURIED ALIVE!

by Jacqueline Wilson

Tim's diary

Biscuits's diary

This is my holiday diary. Whoops. My writing is a bit wobbly because I am in the car. My mum gave Biscuits and me these diaries. There was a red diary and a brown diary. This is the brown one. I really wanted the red but I had to let Biscuits choose first. Biscuits is my best ever friend. I think.

I am going on holiday with my mum and my dad and my friend Biscuits.

WALES

I had a big breakfast with sausages (yum) because I was going on a long journey.

Then we stopped at the motorway cafe and guess what. I had a second big breakfast. With egg and bacon and baked beans and more sausages (yum again)

I spent some of my holiday money in the shop. I got fudge and toffee and a giant choc bar

Toffees   Giant choc bar

And some chocolate biscuits too. In case I get hungry.

I'd been looking forward to my holiday for ages and ages. We were going to this seaside place in Wales called Llanpistyll. It is a funny name. It's spelled funny too. It's in Wales and lots of Welsh words are peculiar. Dad says it's a super place though. He went there when he was a boy.

'We had such fun, me and my brothers,' said Dad. 'We swam every day and we made a camp and we played French cricket on the beach and we went for long clifftop walks.'

'I don't want to go on any clifftop walks,' said Mum. 'I hate it when people go too near the edge.'

'I won't go too near the edge, Mum,' I said.

I hate heights too. I went abseiling once. I had to. It was an adventure holiday. It was s-o-o-o-o scary.*

* *See CLIFFHANGER by Jacqueline Wilson, available in Corgi Yearling paperback.*

55

I am here and guess what. Dad is right. LLanpistyll is brilliant. Biscuits and I get the giggles whenever we say LLanpistyll. We say it a lot. HEAPS of things have happened. Biscuits nearly committed a murder.

Eek!

And I built the Eighth Wonder of the World (miniature version) but then it was destroyed by a <u>Deadly</u> <u>Fiendish</u> <u>Enemy</u>.

D.F.E.'s mate

I squatted down beside my castle and tried to mould it into shape. It was far more finicky that I'd thought. Sand got right up my nails and invaded the legs of my shorts. Little gritty bits embedded themselves in my knees. I tried to fashion a little drawbridge but it was hopeless. My arrow-slit windows weren't exact enough. The tower kept wobbling and collapsing.

'That'll do,' said Biscuits. 'Here, we'll stick little shells in front to make a path, right?'

'You don't have a path. We could make a moat. And fill it with water from the sea.'

We didn't have a bucket so we had to make do with old paper cups. We ran to the sea and filled them up and ran back to the castle and tipped the water in the proposed moat. It immediately disappeared down through the sand.

'Rats,' I said again. I stared at my lop-sided little castle with its empty moat and sighed. 'It's not much of a castle, is it, Biscuits?'

'I think it's a super castle.' said Biscuits. 'Truly. A fantastic creation. Practically the Eighth Wonder of the World. Honest, Tim.'

'Ooooh! Let's see this super-duper castle, eh?' said a loud voice behind us, making us both jump.

★   ★   ★

Two boys had crept up behind us. One was about our age and very pale and pinched-looking. He didn't look very tough but his smile was spiteful. He was the sort of boy you treated with caution.

The other boy was much bigger. And much tougher too. His hair was shaved so short it was just prickles, which looked as sharp as spikes. If he head-butted you you'd get severely perforated. He was the sort of boy that made a Red Alert Alarm system buzz inside your brain.

He was wearing great big Doc Martens even on the beach. I looked at the boy. I looked at the boots. I knew what was going to happen next.

'What a dinky ducky castle you two little cissy boys have made,' he said, his eyes beady. 'Shame it's just sand. Someone could accidentally trip and...'

He kicked hard. The castle collapsed. He laughed. His mate laughed.

Biscuits and I didn't laugh at all.

Prickle-Head and Pinch-Face were going to get us!

RED, WHITE AND BLUE

by Robert Leeson

English
<u>Pen Friend Project</u>

Class Seven
The High School
Meadowbank, Bayfield
Oxon.

7th September

Hi, I'm Wain.

My real name is Gawain (the one who cut off the Green Knight's head off), but mostly I'm called Wain, except by my mother. My brother is called Lance which, as you can guess, is short for Lancelot.

He is five years older than me and a lot bigger. My mother is tall and willowy with green eyes. My grandmother is also tall and stately with white hair. She carries a large blue handbag where she keeps the tablets for my grandfather who is broad and has a red face. They live elsewhere and we see them now and then.

So we are a small family but a big one, if you see what I mean.

Every male in our family for five generations has been a soldier. That is what my grandfather says and he should know. He has a lot of papers about military history and he was very pleased with the new National Curriculum, until they changed it again. I am not sure what he thinks now.

You will notice that I do not mention my father, also very tall, by the way. That is because he is a war hero, or was I mean, in Aden, Anguilla, Belize and Northern Ireland.

But he was missing, believed killed on the shores of the Magellan Strait, south of Rio Gallegos in Argentina. He was leading a raiding party, as a diversion for another raiding party on one of their bases. His party was surrounded, but the other soldiers were able to get away because he covered their retreat. He was never seen again.

That was during the Falklands War and happened before I was born, pretty well. So I have never seen him except in photos. But I know about him from newspaper cuttings. My brother keeps them in a drawer in his room.

When he has finished school and college, he will join the Army and that will make six generations.

In my next letter I'll tell you about my new school, Bayfield High.

22, Croxton Avenue
Bayfield
Oxon., England

9th September

Hi, it's Wain again.

That last lot, on the white paper, was pretty naff, wasn't it? But that was homework. Write to a pen friend or someone and tell them all about yourself.

That's a joke for a start. I don't have a pen friend, or any sort of friend. We only moved to Bayfield in the summer, and I make friends very, very slowly.

So I'm sorry, friend, but you don't exist. But that is no reason why I shouldn't tell you the whole truth, is it?

This red paper is from a writing set my grandparents gave me when I started High School — red, white and blue writing paper, would you believe? I was so embarrassed. I know there are some people who wear red, white and blue vests and boxer shorts. That sends my grandfather spare, and makes my grandmother change the subject. But, paper?

Then I had this inspiration. Keep the white paper for the official version, like homework, which

I have to hand in at school, to the powers that be.

Keep the red paper for the real truth, like when I write to you, unknown friend.

Ah, and the blue paper. That's for my own writing, for my eyes only — a fantasy novel, about a place called Sylvania. It's so confidential that I use the pen name, Gaw Penhallon.

So let's start again.

First, my name. I really like Gawain. But I call myself Wain so as not to attract attention. That is the worst thing you can do in a new school — especially in First Year, I mean Year Seven.

On the white paper I told you ours was a big family. Well, I'm not. I'm vertically challenged, horizontally challenged, diagonally challenged, you name it. I have this weight problem, I don't weigh enough. I read in Biology (which I quite like) that a mature cod is more than a metre long and weighs twenty-eight and a half kilograms. I wouldn't last two rounds with one.

When I was born, my brother was five times as big as me. Eleven years later and he's still twice as big as me, more or less. I know I'll never catch up, so I'm just hanging on until he joins the Army.

The truth is, my brother's a thug.

When my father... didn't come back, he left some things behind, like a cricket bat, rugby ball and so on. My mother who is very fair, divided it all up between my brother and me.

But as soon as he could, my brother took everything — I mean every single thing, as well as all the photos and the bits out of the newspapers, up to his room.

He'd have taken Father's medals but my mother keeps those in a case in her room.

I have said nothing about this daylight robbery of my brother's, and it is not out of loyalty. If I did say anything, he would give me a Chinese burn or a kidney punch or lift me up by the hair. I like my hair long, but now I have it cut short just to make things difficult for him.

I keep out of his way and that isn't easy in a small house like ours. I wish we had a big old ramshackle house like my grandparents', with cellars and attics and old cupboards and wardrobes you could disappear into — and maybe never come back.

So I'm hanging on until my brother leaves home, which is another year, and I have this feeling it is going to be the worst year of my life — so far. I daren't look further ahead.

HANNAH GOSLAR REMEMBERS

by Alison Leslie Gold

At age thirteen Hannah Goslar was fun-loving but also quite religious. She went to Hebrew school two times a week and to synagogue. She was gangly, tall, had creamy skin, and brushed her mahogany brown hair so fast that electric sparks crackled. Hannah's best features were her soft, brown eyes.

This morning she was going to call for her friend Anne Frank. Anne was outspoken, even impudent; she loved having fun. She was more interested in socializing and boyfriends than Hebrew lessons. Lately the differences between Hannah and Anne had become more pronounced. With the war raging and both of them being thirteen, life was not as simple as it used to be when they were little girls sitting side by side at school.

Hannah had kissed her father before she left the house. Because of a new law that Jews were forbidden from working in most professions, Mr. Goslar was no longer allowed to work as a professional economist. This meant it was difficult for him to support his family.

Broken Sky

by Chris Wooding

ACT ONE, PART ONE

Ty was still. He had never been this close to an untethered wyvern. His eyes ranged nervously over its huge form as it regarded him with an intelligent gaze. Its skin was a leathery black, but its head, back, chest and the upper side of its wings were covered in rigid white plates of a bone-like armour. It stood on two legs, with inverted knees like those of a horse and massive three-toed claws. A long, snake-like neck ended in a blunt, rounded muzzle of black, surrounded by a skull-like mask of white bone. Its eyes were a bright amber, and no pupils swam inside them.

"What's it called?" he breathed.

Kia laughed, a high, cascading sound. The wyvern's head curled round on its long neck to look at her. "I don't know. We don't name them unless they're Bonded."

"It's got to be... Hey, what's going on?"

Ty was midway through his sentence when

suddenly there was a ripple of collective movement across the roost, a synchronized action like a flock of birds taking off together. As one, every wyvern in the roost had suddenly looked up, and had either stopped still or were lazily gliding to a perch.

Suddenly, there was a blast of explosive air as the nearby wyvern launched off the ledge, swooping down into the depths of the canyon and disappearing into one of the caves. The rest of the wyverns were following suit; after a few moments the frenzied sound of movement died into silence, and the roost was deserted.

"What was that all about?" Ty asked Kia, his eyes ranging nervously across the cave mouths.

"Something's frightened them," Kia said, concern in her voice as she looked up at the sky.

"Wait..." said Ty, following her gaze. "I think I can hear something..."

Over the soft hiss of the breeze, a swooshing noise was approaching, gradually getting louder. "What is that?" Ty asked, the question addressed to nobody in particular.

He was answered by an ear-shattering screech, and three wyverns exploded over the mountain tops, screaming by overhead. Ty shuddered, his hands flying to his ears.

LOUD EMILY

by Alexis O'Neill
(Abridged extract)

From the moment of birth Emily's voice
boomed.

"GOO GOO BA BA!" Emily sang in her
Emily voice.

It startled the midwife. It astonished the
neighbours. It frightened the birds that were
nesting in trees.

Emily's parents loved her truly, but oh, dear!
Her voice could be heard 'round that seaside
town!

"Perhaps she'll grow out of it," said her
father as he closed all the windows and fastened
the doors.

"We can only hope," said her mother as she covered her ears with embroidered pillows.

But as Emily grew, so did her voice. It rattled the brasses. It shimmied the crystals. It shattered the plates as they crashed to the floor.

"**GOOD MORNING!**" Emily said in her Emily voice.

"Please be soft," said Father.

"**GOOD AFTERNOON!**" Emily said in her Emily voice.

"What about a boarding school?" her father wondered.

"A boarding school?" her mother asked.

"Yes, she must go to a boarding school," crowed the tutor, "far across the sea! And may I suggest Miss Meekmeister's School for Soft-Spoken Girls?"

Emily tried to be happy. But a misty greyness crept inside her and would not go away.

On the day before Emily was to set sail, the cook took her hand. "Come, little Emily. Before you go, come with me to Front Street and help me buy some nice fresh fish."

Emily heard Front Street before she saw it. Oh! What a lovely place it was, there among the tall ships. The salty air rang with the sounds of riggers and smithies and coopers at work. Sailors trundled cargo along wooden wharves. Carriages thundered up cobblestone streets. Crowds burst from taverns with songs on their lips.

"I LOVE IT HERE!" Emily said in her Emily voice. As Emily skipped along the wharf, she saw a small notice tacked to a large ship.

LOUD HELP NEEDED.

NOW.

CASTING OFF TODAY.

Captain Baroo

"Ahoy there," called the first mate to Emily. "Are you loud?"

"I AM!" answered Emily.

"Come aboard, then," he said.

And Emily did.

Captain Baroo's crew was kind and luckless. But how they loved Emily's voice! She sang halyard shanties while hoisting the sails. She called bosun's commands while standing watch. She told stories to the crew while swabbing the deck. From her tidy bunk at night she crooned foícísle ballads that made the men cry.

And deep out in the ocean the whales listened, too. They danced to her wild tunes.

They sang with her free songs. They spouted and blew their delight in the air.

One day, a storm lifted waves into walls of water and shivered the timbers of the very old ship. Captain Baroo whispered commands into Emily's ear.

Emily shouted, **"AVAST! LUFF HER UP BEFORE WE'RE STOVE!"**

But when morning came, fog rolled in like a blanket of blubber.

"Can't see a thing!" complained Captain Baroo.

"Neither can we!" moaned his poor tired crew, and they fell fast asleep on the deck.

Emily peered over the railing.

Rocks! The ship was racing fast toward a rough, jagged shore. Where was the lighthouse? Had the fierce storm destroyed it?

"AHOY!" Emily called in her Emily voice. **"AHOY! AHOY!"** But nothing could wake the snoring crew. She pulled at the tiller but the ship wouldn't turn. What could she do?

And then she remembered the whales.

Emily rushed to the bowsprit and shimmied along. Into the waves she cast her voice until a ribbon of bubbles carried her words into the briny deep: **"DANGER! PLEASE HELP! DANGER! PLEASE HELP!"** She sang in song for the whales. And as Emily sang, the whales gathered around. They hastened from Baja, they raced from Iceland, they speeded their way from the tip of Cape Horn. Then, as if the ship were one of their own, they nuzzled her and cradled her and eased her away from the treacherous coast.

Soon the sun shone in the wide sky. On the horizon were ships and ships and ships, far from the threatening rocks. Along the shore stood all the folks of the city shouting **HURRAH!** for the little girl with the very big voice. The happiest shouts of all came from her own proud parents.

Now Emily lives with her parents in a home near the lighthouse on top of the rocks. On sunny days Emily does what little girls do. But on foggy days, and on stormy days, and on very windy days, Emily cautions all ships in her loudest Emily voice and keeps them safe from harm.

And nobody there in that house by the sea ever complains of the noise.

THE RUNNER

by Keith Gray

It wasn't running away. Not proper running away. Not really.

The monster Intercity hauled itself into the station. Jason was already at the edge of the platform with his bag in his hand. The other waiting passengers crowded round him as the train slowed. He kept his head low, scared someone might recognise him, and gripped the handles of his bag tighter. It felt so very heavy, it seemed to be dragging him down. Could he really carry it all the way to Liverpool? After as many as eight or nine carriages the train finally managed to bring itself to a halt. It still had another two or three to go but left them hanging out of the station, like a tall man in a small bed. The straggly crowd was an excuse not to queue and Jason was the last to climb aboard, even though he'd been one of the first waiting.

He followed the crowd on to the train and grabbed the first empty seat he came to. Then almost immediately wished he hadn't. Sitting across the aisle from him was an elderly woman with a bag of Mint Imperials and a wrinkly smile. She offered him first the smile, then a sweet. He shook his head quickly and hurried through to the next carriage along, lugging his bag behind him. The woman looked just like his Auntie Jen, who Michael had always called the nosiest woman in the world. But this carriage was better, just some businessmen who seemed far too interested in their morning papers to wonder what an eleven-year-old boy was doing travelling so far by himself.

He sat by the window and let his bag block the seat next to him. He checked his watch. Nine twenty-seven; the train left at half past. He was surprised by just how hard and fast his heart was beating and zipped his jacket right up under his chin to try to help keep the noise in, then folded his arms over his chest too.

He began humming a tune to himself nervously. At first he thought he was making it up. He hated himself when he realised it was one of the songs that his father always played and forced it quickly out of his head. He thought of something by Oasis instead, because they were Michael's favourite band, and waited for the train to get going.

Amber Brown
is Feeling Blue

by Paula Danziger

When I was growing up, I hated my name, hated being teased about being the shade of a crayon, and I never would have dressed as a crayon.

Now that I'm in fourth grade, I, Amber Brown, am proud of my name.

It's a very colourful name for a very colourful person... That's what my mom always tells me. I like having a unique name, one that no one else has. That's why I made my costume.

I forget what I'm wearing and start to sit down on the sofa. It doesn't work.

The only problem with being dressed as a crayon is that it is very hard to sit down and it's a pain to keep taking it off so for the past four hours I've been standing. Actually, there is another problem about being dressed as a crayon, but I don't want to talk about it because it has to do with trying to go to the bathroom.

I, Amber Brown, am one very tired crayon.

GOGGLE-EYES

by Anne Fine

Kitty Killin is not only a good story teller but also the World's Greatest Expert when it comes to mothers having new and unwanted boyfriends, particularly when there's the danger they might turn into new and unwanted stepfathers. That's why she's the one who is sent down to talk to Helly Johnston in the dark privacy of the Lost Property cupboard. And why she tells Helly the story of her mum and Gerald Faulkner, also known as Goggle-eyes, once the most unwanted boyfriend of them all...

I know a storm warning when I hear one. On Thursday I was determined to make sure that there'd be nothing in the bad manners line that she could pin on me. When he rang the doorbell I made as if I simply hadn't heard, so it was Jude who reached the door to let him in, while I stood in the shadow at the bottom of the stairs.

He stepped inside. He was Mum's height, a little tubby, and he had silvery hair. His suit was nowhere near as smart as any of Simon's. There again, he wasn't a posh banker, though he did have the most enormous box of chocolates tucked under one arm.

He shifted the chocolates, and shook hands.

'Judith,' he said. 'Right?'

She nodded. I sidled out of the shadow.

'And Kitty.'

He smiled, and kept his hand stuck out for a moment, but I pretended that I hadn't noticed it. And after one of those infinitesimal little pauses of his, he handed the huge box of chocolates to Jude.

They were those rich, dark, expensive, chocolate-coated cream mints. I've had a passion for them all my life. The box was three layers deep at the very least. I saw Jude's eyes widen to saucers.

'Are these for Mum?' she asked.

'No. They're for you.'

He could have meant either *you*, or *you two*. It wasn't clear. As he spoke, he was looking at Jude, but he did glance at me briefly. It was terribly clever. It meant that when I didn't pile straight in with Jude, thanking him lavishly, he wasn't in the slightest embarrassed. He didn't have to be, you see. He might not have meant to include me at all.

'I'll tell Mum.'

Jude rushed upstairs, clutching her booty to

her chest, and Gerald Faulkner and I were left alone in the hall. I thought I'd discomfit him with my silence, but no, not at all. He simply swivelled away as though he wanted to inspect the pictures on the wall, and peered closely at a photo of me as a toddler.

'What a face!' he said admiringly. (I wasn't quite sure what he meant by that.) 'It looks as if it might be you.'

Really cunning, right? He doesn't actually *ask* if it's me, and then he can't look silly if I don't answer.

Just then Floss padded in through the front door, and started rubbing up against his trouser legs as if she'd known and loved him all her life. He stopped to pet her. 'Puss, puss, puss.' I thought now he'd be bound to try and get me to speak. It's hard to fondle someone else's cat in front of them, and not ask its name. But Gerald Faulkner's made of sterner stuff than that.

'Up you come, Buster,' he said, scooping Floss up in his arms. 'Who's a *nice* Kitty?'

I wasn't quite sure what he meant by that, either. I was still trying to work it out (and Floss was still purring shamelessly) when Jude came thundering downstairs.

'Mum says to help yourself to a drink, and

she'll be down in a minute.'

'Right-ho.'

He tipped the enraptured Floss into Jude's arms, and ambled past me with a nod. I realised that he must have been in our house at least once before. How else would he know which door led into the kitchen? Jude padded after him like a pet dog, and I was forced to lean back against the door frame so I didn't look ridiculous, standing there doggedly staring the other way.

He stood at one end of the cabinets and opened the first two doors, looked in, then closed them. He moved along and did the same again, and again. I said nothing, just leaned against the door frame and watched. But Jude caught on before he'd gone very much further.

'Do you want glasses? They're in here.'

And she rushed about, finding him the only sharp knife, and a lemon, and groping about on the floor for a couple of ice-cubes that slithered off the table. The two of them kept up a steady chat about nothing at all – how quickly bottled drinks lose their fizz, how long it takes for water to freeze in an ice tray. I was astonished. Jude's not a talker, on the whole. It's like the business of the telephone. She can go hours without bothering. But here she was, burbling away merrily to this perfect stranger.

He only spoke to me directly once. He'd just pushed my school bag further along the table to keep it safe from a small puddle of melted ice. The bag was open and my books were showing – not just *France Aujourd'hui* and *Modern Mathematics*, but also the things I'm reading on the bus and at bedtime: *A Thousand Worst Jokes* and that thriller *Coma*, about a hospital where the anaesthesia goes haywire.

He tapped the jacket of *Coma* with his knuckle.

'Is this a book about punctuation?' he asked me. 'Because, if it is, the author can't spell.'

I couldn't resist.

'A pity the other book isn't *A Thousand and One Worst Jokes*,' I snapped. 'You could have offered them yours.'

There. I had spoken to him. I had done my bit. So I turned on my heel and walked out of the kitchen.

Mum was half-way down the stairs, wearing a frilly blouse and smart velvet trousers. I glowered at her and, misunderstanding, she said:

'Listen, I'm really sorry about missing the meeting tonight.'

'Missing the meeting?'

This was him. He had sneaked up behind me with the tray. On it four glasses fizzed, tinkling with ice, and I could smell the tang of lemons.

Mum took the glass he offered her, and smiled at him.

'Kitty and I always go together on Thursdays,' she explained. 'She's a bit cross because, now I'm not coming, she'll have to take the bus.'

I *hate* it when people just assume they know the reasons for everything. I don't mind taking the bus. I never have. I like Mum to come because our car ride together to the meeting is about the only time – the *only* time – I'm sure I've got her on my own. That's one of the worst things about Dad moving away to Berwick upon Tweed. Jude and I hardly ever get to be alone with him or with Mum. We're either both with the one or we're both with the other. And they can't split themselves in two, so one of us can have a private chat down the back garden while the other is pouring out her heart on the sofa.

I was about to say 'I am *not cross*' when Gerald Faulkner touched my elbow with his, proffering his tray.

'Here,' he said, nodding at the closest glass. 'That one's yours.'

Without thinking, I lifted the drink off the tray. I could have kicked myself. In spite of all the effort he'd put in to making them, I had intended to refuse mine. But at least I could still refuse to say thank you. Unfortunately, just as Mum opened her mouth to prompt me, he waved his hand as if to cut off all the profuse and gracious thanks on which he was sure I was going to embark any second, and said, as if I were *eighteen*, or something:

'I didn't put any alcohol in yours because I didn't know if you liked the taste.'

That threw Mum. She doesn't like anyone even to suggest within ten miles of my hearing that, one day, I might be old enough to go to a pub without being sent home to bed by the landlord. For someone to imply, even if only out of tact and politeness, that I might be on the verge of growing out of fizzy lemonade, well, that was more than she could handle. Changing the subject as fast as she could, she plucked at the frilly blouse and the velvet trousers, and asked us both:

'Are these all right?'

'Yes,' I said. 'They're all right.' (I was still mad.)

She turned to him.

'Gerald?'

He put his head on one side. 'They're lovely,' he said. 'Absolutely smashing. You look tremendous. But won't you spoil me a little? Wear the blue suit with those tiny wooden toggle fasteners, the black diamond stockings and the shiny bow shoes.'

I stared. I absolutely *stared*. Was he some wardrobe pervert, or something? Dad lived with her for years, and he could no more have described any of her clothes like that than flown up in the air. In fact, I don't think Dad even noticed what Mum wore. Obviously if she came down the stairs all tarted up to go out somewhere special, he'd say, 'Oh, you look very nice.' But ask her to go back up and change into something he liked even better? You have to be *joking*.

And her? Blush and shrug, and turn round to trot obediently back upstairs to change, holding her glass high? Was this my mum?

Smart Answers for
SUPERKIDS

by Laurence Anholt

Illustrated by Martin Chatterton

A SUPERKID is a walking dictionary
of corny jokes and smart answers that can
be used in almost any situation...

You see? It's not difficult.
Why not go and practise straight away?
The kitchen is a good place to start...

You get the idea? Even when ill a **SUPERKID** has a smart answer...

The Weird Files

ZOMBIE ZONE EARTH

by Michael Johnstone

'Prepare yourself, Con,' Frick sneered. Prepare yourself for memory oblivion treatment, followed by a long sleep. A very, very long sleep!'

I refused to give him the satisfaction of witnessing my terror. So I simply stared at him, watching his every move as he turned the dials on the box first one way, then another, as if he was opening one of the old safes we had mucked about with in History of Technology Class at PEC 815.

I had never much liked the dump, but I would have given my eye teeth to be back there now with dull old Anders and mean old Gwaina.

I watched him press several buttons and flick three switches. Then he nodded at another Guardian who was standing by a large lever set in the wall. The moment he pulled it, I heard a slight crackling sound as the end of each wire started to glow.

Within seconds I felt as if I was being wrapped in a smooth velvet blanket that was smothering me in its soft warmth.

What now? I thought to myself, as my eyes grew heavier and heavier.

'Sleep!' Frick's voice drifted into my head. 'Close your eyes and give yourself up to Morpheus. Surrender to sleep and forget all that has gone before.'

As he spoke the soles of my feet began to feel as if they were being gently bathed in warm water, and then started to go numb as the warmth crept up my legs and into my body, and I became drowsier and drowsier with every second that passed.

'That's it,' Frick's voice now sounded as soothing as the warmth. 'Surrender to sleep.'

It was then that I heard another voice, a woman's, but one I didn't recognise.

'Fight,' it whispered urgently. 'You must fight.'

Fight! I thought. I must fight. I tried to stop the warmth flooding over me. I tried to will normal feeling back into my body. I tried to keep my eyes open.

"Fight it,' I heard myself shouting out aloud. 'I've got to fight it.'

'You can't possibly fight it, Con.' Frick's voice was harsh now.

'I can,' I cried. 'I must.'

But it was no good. Even as I spoke, my eyes began to close as I drifted off to where old Morpheus was waiting to wrap me in his arms.

'He is ready.' Frick's voice cut through my drowsiness. 'Begin the memory oblivion treatment.'

'Treatment... Treatment... Treatment.' The word bounced round my brain like a rubber ball. And when it stopped, in my mind's eye I saw myself trapped in my glass tomb, floating backwards out of the room I was in, out along the corridor, and upwards to the ceiling.

I heard the sound of a thousand voices murmuring something I could not really understand before I was raised upright, and the panels of my coffin slid back into the roof.

Now I was floating down towards an escort of waiting Guardians who marched me back to the room where I had struggled against the Guardians and jerked Frick's airtubes from his face. I felt a glow of satisfaction as I relived the scene in my mind.

'That's it,' Frick's voice intruded harshly on my thoughts again. 'Remember everything. Every detail of your life.'

I drifted backwards in time.

Boo!

by Kevin Crossley-Holland

She didn't like it at all when her father had to go down to London and, for the first time, she had to sleep alone in the old house.

She went up to her bedroom early. She turned the key and locked the door. She latched the windows and drew the curtains. She peered inside her wardrobe, and pulled open the bottom drawer of her chest-of-drawers; she got down on her knees and looked under the bed.

She undressed; she put on her nightdress.

She pulled back the heavy linen cover and climbed into bed. Not to read but to try and sleep – she wanted to sleep as soon as she could. She reached out and turned off the lamp.

'That's good,' said a little voice. 'Now we're safely locked in for the night.'

THE GHOST HOUSE

by Marie Birkenshaw

This is the scream
that comes from the train
when we see the face
that follows the hand,
that shakes the chain,
that rattles the train,
that rumbles the floor,
as it goes through the door
to the ghost house.

Supposing...

by Frances Thomas

'Mummy,' said Little Monster.

'Supposing when I woke up tomorrow morning... supposing there was a big... black... hole in the middle of the floor. And I didn't want to fall in it so I called you and you didn't answer. And then supposing the hole got bigger and bigger and it was all dark and smelly. And then there was a big, big spider and it got closer and closer. And then there wasn't a ceiling and the sky was all horrible and I fell down and down and down. And supposing you couldn't come and help me because you had gone away. And then the house went on fire! And all the fire was round me when I was falling down the hole. And the spider was falling too and I couldn't see the bottom of the hole and I just went on falling forever and ever and ever. Mummy, supposing all that happened when I woke up tomorrow, what would it be like?'

'Mmm,' said Mother Monster, 'that would be very scary. But then supposing tomorrow when you woke up, you called me and I was making pancakes. And supposing you ate up all your pancakes, and then we went for a walk. And supposing we walked and walked until we found a green hill. And at the bottom of the hill was an old man with a long red scarf, selling balloons. And supposing I bought a red balloon like a red jewel, and you bought a green balloon like the green sea, and a blue balloon like the blue sky...'

'And a purple balloon,' said the little monster, 'like... like a lovely purple balloon.'

'Like a lovely purple balloon,' said Mother.

'And then supposing you and I climbed all the way to the top of the hill, and we stood there in the sun, and then I let my red balloon float away and away into the sky. And then you let your blue balloon float away and away and your green balloon.'

'Only not my purple balloon,' said Little Monster. 'I would take my purple balloon back home with me.'

'Oh yes,' said Mother Monster. 'We'd take your purple balloon home. But then on the way we'd meet an old man with a long yellow scarf, selling ice-creams. And supposing you had strawberry and I had chocolate...'

'Or the other way round?' said Little Monster.

COULD YOU BE A VILE VOLCANOLOGIST?

by Anita Ganeri

Do you have what it takes to become a vile volcanologist? Try this quick quiz to find out.

1 Do you have a head for heights? Yes/No
2 Are you fabulously fit and strong? Yes/No
3 A hot photographer? Yes/No
4 Do you look good in a gas mask? Yes/No

DOES ANYONE?

5 Can you tell the date from a tree ring? Yes/No

ER...IS IT JUNE 24?

6 Do you know your rocks? Yes/No

Answers:

1 You'll need one – some volcanoes are horribly high. It's a very long way up the world's highest active volcano – Guallatiri in Chile's 6,060 metres high. Its last major eruption was in 1987.

2 You'll need to be – there's a lot of hard climbing involved (see above). If you're woefully weak and feeble, you'll never be able to carry all your horribly heavy equipment. Or the even heavier heaps of rock. Time to build those muscles up!

3 Not essential but useful for showing off afterwards.

4 Like it or not, you'll have to wear one. Volcanoes give off lots of gas, most of it horribly poisonous. And collecting gas samples is a major part of your job.

5 Handy if you can. One of a volcanologist's jobs is finding out about past eruptions. Which might give you a clue to a volcano's future. One way of doing this is to look inside a tree. Each year the trunk grows a new ring.

6 If you can't tell your basalt from your bath salts, you'll be no good to anyone. As every good volcanologist knows basalt is an igneous (fire) rock made when lava cools.

HARRY POTTER
and the Philosopher's Stone

by J. K. Rowling

Harry took the wand. He felt a sudden warmth in his fingers. He raised the wand above his head, brought it swishing down through the dusty air and a stream of red and gold sparks shot from the end like a firework, throwing dancing spots of light on to the walls. Mr Ollivander cried, 'Oh bravo! Yes, indeed, oh, very good. Well, well, well... how curious... how very curious...'

He put Harry's wand back into its box and wrapped it in brown paper, still muttering, 'Curious... curious...'

'Sorry,' said Harry, 'but what's curious?'

Mr Ollivander fixed Harry with his pale stare.

'I remember every wand I've ever sold, Mr Potter. Every single wand. It so happens that the phoenix whose tail feather is in your wand, gave another feather – just one other. It is very curious indeed that you should be destined for this wand when its brother – why, its brother gave you that scar.'

The Amazing Adventures of SOUPY BOY!

by Damon Burnard

LOOK! See that THING streaking across the sky? Is it a bird? Is it a plane? Is it a custard pie thrown by a very strong and angry clown?

NO! It's none of these! It's...

SOUPY BOY, SOUPER HERO!

Here he is from closer up...

"Gosh!" I hear you say. "Just who *is* this mysterious souper being?" Well, make yourself comfortable and prepare to hear a tale which will ASTONISH and AMAZE!

Meet Ashley Fugg. Twelve years ago this cute baby had a TERRIBLE ACCIDENT...

On a visit to a soup factory with his parents, he fell into a vat of tomato soup!

Into the soup the daring diver dove. HOWEVER, this wasn't just any old soup, oh no! Unknown to all, this soup was infected by RADIOACTIVE COSMIC DUST! And so, by the time Ashley was fished out, he'd mutated into...

Growing up as a tin of soup was tough and lonely. Kids at school could be mean and gruel. I mean cruel...

But deep inside, Ashley felt something stirring; something no-one else could share or understand. For during his mutation had been sown the seeds of SPECIAL POWERS!

Day by day, the force grew stronger and stronger until, with a twirl and a spin, Ashley could transform into...

Here are just a few of Soupy Boy's souper powers...

He CAN FLY! (Whee!)

He CAN ROLL downhill QUICKLY... (Help!)

He CAN HEAR AROUND CORNERS! (Nice day!) (Gasp! 'Mice pay'? What can he mean?)

WHAT'S MORE he can TRANSFORM himself into any kind of soup he wishes! For example...

Lentil

Chicken noodle (Puss!)

Bird's nest (Oh, funny ha, ha...)

Ashley decided to keep his identity a secret, and to use these INCREDIBLE POWERS for the benefit of all humankind. He decided to become...

A CRIMEFIGHTER!

Luckily, there are plenty of criminals to keep Soupy Boy busy. Cheats and villains like...

Evan Nose — sniff!
Lionel Dangle — Grr! Toot!
The Tooter

But right now, he's on the trail of the sick and twisted MORTIMER NAPKIN!

Sick and twisted? Me?
Watch your mouth!

Will Soupy Boy win the day for JUSTICE and FREEDOM? Or will

Mortimer's EVIL GENIUS crush him like a BUG? It's up to you, Fearless Reader, to find out! So if you've got the stomach for sizzling suspense, hilarious jokes and mind-blowing puzzles, check out

The Amazing Adventures of SOUPY BOY!

BZ≡≡JJJOO! Later, dudes!

And look out for Damon Burnard's fantastic new graphic novel, 'Burger!', coming in June!

SERIOUSLY SILLY STORIES
LITTLE RED RIDING WOLF

by Laurence Anholt

In the very darkest corner of the deep dark wood sat the Big Bad Girl.

The Big Bad Girl was just about as BIG and BAD as a girl can be, and all the woodland animals were afraid of her. She hung about beside the forest path and carved her name on trees. She shouted rude things at any little animal who passed by. The Big Bad Girl tripped up little deer. She stole fir cones from baby squirrels and threw them at the poor little hedgehogs. The woodland birds didn't dare to sing when the Big Bad Girl was around! But the person the Big Bad Girl liked to tease most of all was a charming little wolf cub who often passed by on his way to visit his dear Old Granny Wolf.

Little Wolfie was the sweetest, fluffiest, politest little cub you could ever hope to meet. He would run along the path, skippety-skip, carrying a basket of freshly baked goodies for Old Granny Wolf, singing all the time...

I'm a little wolfie, good and sweet.
I am tidy, I am neat.
With a basket full of lovely grub,
I am Granny's favourite cub.

"Wot's in yer basket today, Little-Weedy-Wolfie-Wimp?" snarled the Big Bad Girl. "Mmmm, apple pies? I'll take those. Jam sandwiches? Very tasty."

"Oh dear, oh dear! Now there will be nothing for dear Old Granny Wolf," wailed Little Wolfie. And his little wolfie tears rolled into the empty basket.

Poetry

"Poetry = the best words in the best order."
Samuel Taylor Coleridge 1827

BIG BAD RAPS

by
Tony
Mitton

Just on the edge
of a deep, dark wood
lived a girl called
Little Red Riding Hood.
Her grandmother lived
not far away,
so Red went to pay her
a visit one day...

And the Big Bad Wolf,
who knew her plan
he turned his nose
and ran and ran.
He ran till he came
to her grandmother's door.

Then he locked her up
with a great big roar.
He took her place
in her nice warm bed,
and he waited there
for Little Miss Red.

The Meeting

Adapted by Derek Dwyer

He was standing in our garden,
Looked at me and asked my name.
Told me once he used to live here,
but it didn't look the same.

He was glad we'd kept the apple tree.
He was happy now he'd been.
Said that I could tell my mum
I'd met a man called Sammy Green.

When I told my mum, her face went white;
She didn't say a lot.
I didn't ask her what was wrong,
I thought I'd better not.

But when I was in the graveyard,
I think I found out why.
I found the grave of Sammy Green...
And an apple tree nearby.

PLEASE MRS BUTLER

by Allan Ahlberg

Please Mrs Butler
This boy Derek Drew
Keeps copying my work, Miss.
What shall I do?

Go and sit in the hall, dear.
Go and sit in the sink.
Take your books on the roof, my lamb.
Do whatever you think.

Please Mrs Butler
This boy Derek Drew
Keeps taking my rubber, Miss.
What shall I do?

Keep it in your hand, dear.
Hide it up your vest.
Swallow it if you like, my love.
Do what you think best.

Please Mrs Butler
This boy Derek Drew
Keeps calling me rude names, Miss.
What shall I do?

Lock yourself in the cupboard, dear.
Run away to sea.
Do whatever you can, my flower.
But *don't ask me!*

The Tummy Beast

by Roald Dahl

'One afternoon I said to mummy,
"Who is this person in my tummy?
"He must be small and very thin
"Or how could he have gotten in?"
My mother said from where she sat,
"It isn't nice to talk like that."
"It's true!" I cried. "I swear it, mummy!
"There *is* a person in my tummy!
"He talks to me at night in bed,
"He's always asking to be fed,
"Throughout the day, he screams at me,
"Demanding sugar buns for tea.
"He tells me it is not a sin
"To go and raid the biscuit tin.
"I know quite well it's awfully wrong
"To guzzle food the whole day long,
"But really I can't help it, mummy,
"Not with this person in my tummy."
"You horrid child!" my mother cried.
"Admit it right away, you've lied!
"You're simply trying to produce
"A silly asinine excuse!

"You *are* the greedy guzzling brat!
"And that is why you're always fat!"
I tried once more, "*Believe me*, mummy,
"There *is* a person in my tummy."
"I've had enough!" my mother said,
"You'd better go at once to bed!"
Just then, a nicely timed event
Delivered me from punishment.
Deep in my tummy something stirred,
And then an awful noise was heard,
A snorting grumbling grunting sound
That made my tummy jump around.
My darling mother nearly died.
"My goodness, what was that?" she cried.
At once, the tummy voice came through,
It shouted, "Hey there! Listen you!
"I'm getting hungry! I want eats!
"I want lots of chocs and sweets!
"Get me half a pound of nuts!
"Look snappy or I'll twist your guts!"
"*That's him!*" I cried. "*He's in my tummy*!
"So now do you believe me, mummy?"

But mummy answered nothing more,
For she had fainted on the floor.

What Teachers Wear in Bed!

by Brian Moses

It's anybody's guess
what teachers wear in bed at night,
so we held a competition
to see if any of us were right.

We did a spot of research,
although some of them wouldn't say,
but it's probably something funny
as they look pretty strange by day.

Our headteacher's quite old-fashioned,
he wears a Victorian nightshirt,
our sports teacher wears her tracksuit
and sometimes her netball skirt.

That new teacher in the infants
wears bedsocks with see-through pyjamas,
our deputy head wears a T-shirt
he brought back from the Bahamas.

We asked our secretary what she wore
but she shooed us out of her room,
and our teacher said, her favourite nightie
and a splash of expensive perfume.

And Mademoiselle, who teaches French,
is really very rude,
she whispered, 'Alors! Don't tell a soul,
but I sleep in the... back bedroom!'

Magic Cat
by Peter Dixon

My mum whilst walking through the door
spilt some magic on the floor.
Blobs of this
and splots of that
but most of it upon the cat.

Our cat turned magic, straight away
and in the garden went to play
where it grew two massive wings
and flew around in fancy rings.
'Oh look!' cried Mother, pointing high,
'I didn't know our cat could fly.'
Then with a dash of Tibby's tail
she turned my mum into a snail!

So now she lives beneath a stone
and dusts around a different home.
And I'm an ant
and Dad's a mouse
and Tibby's living in our house.

Timothy Winters

by Charles Causley

Timothy Winters comes to school
With eyes as wide as a football pool,
Ears like bombs and teeth like splinters:
A blitz of a boy is Timothy Winters.

His belly is white, his neck is dark,
And his hair is an exclamation mark.
His clothes are enough to scare a crow
And through his britches the blue winds blow.

When teacher talks he won't hear a word
And he shoots down dead the arithmetic-bird,
He licks the patterns off his plate
And he's not even heard of the Welfare State.

Timothy Winters has bloody feet
And he lives in a house on Suez Street,
He sleeps in a sack on the kitchen floor
And they say there aren't boys like him any more.

Old Man Winters likes his beer
And his missus ran off with a bombardier,
Grandma sits in the grate with a gin
And Timothy's dosed with an aspirin.
The Welfare Worker lies awake
But the law's as tricky as a ten-foot snake,
So Timothy Winters drinks his cup
And slowly goes on growing up.

At Morning Prayers the Master helves★
For children less fortunate than ourselves,
And the loudest response in the room is when
Timothy Winters roars 'Amen!'

So come one angel, come on ten:
Timothy Winters says 'Amen
Amen amen amen amen.'
Timothy Winters, Lord.
    Amen.

★ helves: a dialect word from north Cornwall used to
describe the alarmed lowing of cattle (as when a cow is
separated from her calf); a desperate, pleading note.

HAIRCUT RAP

by Valerie Bloom

Ah sey, ah want it short,
Short back an' side,
Ah tell him man, ah tell him
When ah teck him aside,
Ah sey, ah want a haircut
Ah can wear with pride,
So lef' it long on top
But short back an' side.

Ah sey try an' put a pattern
In the shorter part,
Yuh could put a skull an' crossbone,
Or an arrow through a heart,
Meck sure ah have enough hair lef'
Fe cover me wart,
Lef' a likkle pon the top,
But the res' — keep it short.

Well, bwoy, him start to cut,
An' me settle down to wait,
Him was cuttin' from seven
Till half-past eight,
Ah was startin' to get worried
Cause ah see it gettin' late,
But then him put the scissors down,
Sey, 'There yuh are, mate.'

Well, ah did see a skull an' a
Criss-cross bone or two,
But was me own skull an' bone
That was peepin' through,
Ah look jus' like a monkey
Ah did see once at the zoo,
Him sey, 'What's de matter, Tammy,
Don't yuh like the hair-do?'

Well, ah feel me heart stop beatin'
When me look pon me reflection,
Ah feel like somet'ing frizzle up
Right in me middle section,
Ah look aroun' fe somewhey
Ah could crawl into an' hide
The day ah mek me brother cut
Me hair short back an' side.

This Poem is not...

by Adrian Henri

This poem is not a wolf.

It lives in the depths of forests.
It lurks in the dark where you can't see it.
It hunts in a pack with other poems.
It has big shiny teeth.
It has eyes that glow red in the dark.

This poem is not a wolf.

You won't find it in a zoo,
Though you might find it dressed in sheep's
    clothing
or even disguised as your grandmother.

This poem is not a wolf.

Who's afraid of the big bad poem,
big bad poem, big bad poem?
Who's afraid...
... who?

WORD WHIRLS

by John Foster

On the wheel of words, words whirl, words swirl, words twist, words twirl. Inside the wheel of words, words dance, words spin, words prance, words grin. Words curl, words whirl.

I FEEL SICK!

by Colin McNaughton

Set off before dawn, sick,
Feeling very, yawn, sick,
Wish I'd not been born, sick,

I FEEL SICK!

Is it very far, sick,
Ate a chocolate bar, sick,
Feeling very car-sick,

I FEEL SICK!

Corner of my eye, sick,
Trees are flashing by, sick,
Wish that I could die, sick,

I FEEL SICK!

Dad says look ahead, sick,
Wish that I was dead, sick,
Take me home to bed, sick,

I FEEL SICK!

Queasy, woozy, hot, sick,
My brother says I'm not sick,
Thanks a rotten lot, sick,

I FEEL SICK!

Twisty, turny road, sick,
Chocolate overload, sick,
Ready to explode, sick,

I FEEL SICK!

Daddy, hurry up, sick,
Feel it coming up, sick,
Hic! Hiccup! Hiccup! Sick!

I'VE BEEN SICK!

P.S.

Didn't make the door, sick.
Threw up on the floor, sick.
There isn't any more sick.

I FEEL FINE!

The Mummy

by Shel Silverstein

Wrapped myself in toilet paper,
Head to toe to tummy.
Wrapped myself in toilet paper,
Thought that I'd be funny.
Wrapped myself in toilet paper,
Thought they'd call me "Mummy".
Wrapped myself in toilet paper,
They just call me dummy.

Writer Waiting

by Shel Silverstein

Oh, this shiny new computer –
There just isn't nothin' cuter.
It knows everything the world ever knew.
And with this great computer
I don't need no writin' tutor,
'Cause there ain't a single thing that it can't do.
It can sort and it can spell,
It can punctuate as well.
It can find and file and underline and type.
It can edit and select,
It can copy and correct,
So I'll have a whole book written by tonight
(Just as soon as it can think of *what* to write).

LIMPET

by Ted Hughes

When big surf slams
His tower so hard
The Lighthouse-keeper's
Teeth are jarred.

The Limpet laughs
Beneath her hat:
'There's nothing I love
So much as that!

'Huge seas of shock
That roar to knock me
Off my rocker
Rock me, rock me.'

CRAB

by Ted Hughes

In the low tide pools
I pack myself like
A handy pocket
Chest of tools.

But as the tide fills
Dancing I go
Under lifted veils
Tiptoe, tiptoe.

And with pliers and pincers
Repair and remake
The daintier dancers
The breakers break.

Us Two

by A. A. Milne

Wherever I am, there's always Pooh,
There's always Pooh and Me.
Whatever I do, he wants to do,
"Where are you going today?" says Pooh:
"Well, that's very odd 'cos I was too.
Let's go together," says Pooh, says he.
"Let's go together," says Pooh.

"What's twice eleven?" I said to Pooh,
("Twice what?" said Pooh to Me.)
"I think it ought to be twenty-two."
"Just what I think myself," said Pooh.
"It wasn't an easy sum to do,
But that's what it is," said Pooh, said he.
"That's what it is," said Pooh.

So wherever I am, there's always Pooh,
There's always Pooh and Me.
"What would I do?" I said to Pooh
"If it wasn't for you," and Pooh said: "True,
If it wasn't much fun for One, but Two
Can stick together," says Pooh, says he.
"That's how it is," says Pooh.

ACKNOWLEDGEMENTS

Rules for My Dog by Geraldine Taylor from *Read With Ladybird*, illustrated by Guy Parker Rees, published by Ladybird. From *Mr Croc* by Frank Rogers, published by A & C Black. From *The Old Steam Train* by Heather Amery, illustrated by Stephen Cartwright, published by Usborne Publishing. From *Animorphs 1, The Invasion* by K.A. Applegate, copyright Katherine Applegate 1996, first published in the USA by Scholastic Inc 1996, first published in the UK by Scholastic Ltd 1997. From *The Pet Hotel* by Mandy Archer, published by BBC Worldwide Ltd. From *Little Wolf's Haunted Hall for Small Horrors* by Ian Whybrow, illustrated by Tony Ross, published by Collins Children's Books. *The Jewel* by William Mayne from *The Fox Gate and Other Stories*, illustrated by William Geldart, published by Hodder Children's Books. From *Creatures Book 1, Once I Caught A Fish Alive* by Louise Cooper, copyright Louise Cooper 1998, first published by Scholastic Ltd 1998. From *The Legend of Luke* by Brian Jacques, published by Hutchinson Children's Books, Random House Ltd, copyright The Redwall Abbey Company 1999, reprinted with permission of the publisher. From *Livewires Shakespeare: Romeo and Juliet* edited by Phil Page and Marilyn Pettit, illustrated by Phil Page, reproduced by permission of Hodder and Stoughton Educational, London. From *When Hitler Stole Pink Rabbit* by Judith Kerr published by Collins Children's Books. From *The Awkward Bunch 1, Dead Fishy* by Alex Parsons, copyright Alex Parsons 1999, published by Scholastic Ltd. Extract from *Annie's Game*, published by Corgi Yearling Books, a division of Transworld Publishers Ltd, copyright Narinder Dhami 1999. Extract from *The Wreck of the Zanzibar* by Michael Morpurgo, published by Mammoth, an imprint of Egmont Children's Books, text copyright Michael Morpurgo. Extract from *Buried Alive*, published by Corgi Yearling Books, a division of Transworld Publishers Ltd, text copyright Jacqueline Wilson 1998, illustrations copyright Nick Sharratt and Sue Heap 1998. From *Red, White and Blue* by Robert Leeson published in Collins Cascades by Collins Educational. From *Hannah Goslar Remembers* by Alison Leslie Gold published by Bloomsbury. From *The Broken Sky* by Chris Wooding, copyright Chris Wooding, published by Scholastic. From *Loud Emily* by Alexis O'Neill, illustrated by Nancy Carpenter, published by Simon and Schuster. From *The Runner* by Keith Gray, published by Mammoth, an imprint of Egmont Children's Books, text copyright Keith Gray 1998. From *Amber Brown is Feeling Blue* by Paula Danziger, published by Mammoth, an imprint of Egmont Children's Books, text copyright Paula Danziger 1998,